Animal

GHOST MOUSE

GHOST MOUSE

by Karen Wallace
and Beccy Blake

Evans

First published 2008
Evans Brothers Limited
2A Portman Mansions
Chiltern St
London W1U 6NR

British Library Cataloguing in Publication Data

Wallace, Karen
  Ghost mouse. - (Skylarks)
  1. Children's stories
  I. Title
  823.9'14[J]

ISBN-13: 978 0 23 753582 7 (HB)
ISBN-13: 978 0 23 753594 0 (PB)

Printed in China

Series Editor: Louise John
Design: Robert Walster
Production: Jenny Mulvanny

Contents

Chapter One

A ghost mouse called Gorgonzola was
sleeping in front of a stove. It was a
good life for a mouse. Every night
Granny Flannagan sat in her rocking
chair, read her newspaper and dropped
biscuit crumbs for the mice to nibble.

"Gorgonzola!" squeaked a voice.

"Wake up!"

Gorgonzola opened her eyes. Another ghost mouse called Crackers was staring at her. "Your paw was going in and out of your mouth!"

8

"I was dreaming my favourite dream," murmured Gorgonzola. "About when Granny Flannagan was alive. Before…" her voice trailed away.

Across the room a newspaper lay on the floor. The date on it was October 29th 1897.

"I know all about Granny Flannagan," said Crackers. "She went to the Big Cheese Shop in the sky."

Gorgonzola smiled. "So did we," she said. "And now we're back here to look after Honeycomb Cottage."

"Do you think we'll stay forever?" asked Crackers. "What happens if someone finds the big key?"

"They won't," said Gorgonzola. "When Granny Flannagan died, we hid it, remember?"

At that moment a mouse called
Pipsqueak appeared through the wall.
"Strangers!" he gasped. "And one of
them has got the big key!"

Chapter Two

Melanie Murdock strode into the kitchen and wiped her feet on the precious old newspaper in front of the stove.

"This place is a dump," she said.

Simon Slime of Slime & Slime Estate Agents rubbed his hands together and blushed. "We've only just found the key," he explained. "The cottage has been empty for years and years."

Melanie waved her hands in the air.

"Everything must change! I see arches, patios and huge glass windows."

"We'll get brand new gadgets!" cried Hugo Murdock from under his fluffy golfing hat.

"Absolutely!" cried Melanie as she whacked the stove with her umbrella. "And this will go first."

In the gloomy darkness of her hole, Gorgonzola's heart sank like a turnip in a pond.

"Sniff!" ordered Melanie, suddenly.

"I beg your pardon?" asked Simon Slime.

"I said SNIFF," cried Melanie.

Hugo sniffed. Simon Slime sniffed.

"Can you smell it?" asked Melanie.

"Flowers?" said Simon Slime.

"Pine needles?" said Hugo.

"Mice!" said Melanie. "Fix these."

The ghost mice watched as Simon Slime and Hugo stuck tiny lumps of cheese onto wires sticking out of bits of wood. Then they put them on the floor.

"Perhaps they're trying to be nice to us," said a mouse called Cheddar.

Gorgonzola shook her head. "Those things are mousetraps," she said. "Granny Flannagan never allowed them near Honeycomb Cottage."

"All sorted, sweetest," said Hugo. "Let's come back later."

As soon as they were alone, Gorgonzola turned the mousetraps towards the window, picked up a twig and poked them.

BANG! BANG! BANG! Bits of cheese shot through the air.

"Never forget," said Gorgonzola. "We were here first."

Chapter Three

Gorgonzola opened her eyes sleepily. It was pitch black.

"Gorgonzola!" squeaked Crackers. "Wake up! The strangers came back and blocked up our mouse holes."

"How dare they?" squeaked Gorgonzola. "Where are the others?"

"In the kitchen," said Crackers, "waiting for you."

"Check the traps, Hugo," shouted Melanie as the front door opened. "I'll bring the shopping."

Hugo Murdock walked into the kitchen and peered at the mousetraps.

No cheese. No mice.

"Simon Slime must have been here," he said to himself as he dumped a piece of wood onto the woodpile for the fire.

Gorgonzola gasped. It was the old Honeycomb Cottage sign.

"Well?" asked Melanie.

"No mice," said Hugo. He handed her a parcel. "Here's a surprise for you."

Inside was a plastic sign with the words MELGO MANOR stamped in gold.

"It's a combination of our names," he simpered.

"Wonderful, darling," cried Melanie. She stuck a piece of paper to the wall. "And here are my plans!"

One by one the ghost mice peeped out to get a better look. On the wall was a picture of a very modern house.

There were arches and huge plastic windows everywhere.

"Where's my garage?" asked Hugo.

"In the flower garden," replied Melanie. "Now help me empty the car. There's lots to do before the bulldozers come."

As the door closed, Gorgonzola jumped onto the rocking chair. "Call an emergency meeting!" she squeaked and a second later every ghost mouse in Honeycomb Cottage was there.

"These strangers want to destroy Honeycomb Cottage," cried Gorgonzola. "We've got to get rid of them!"

"How?" wailed a tiny silver mouse.

"We'll scare them away, of course," cried Gorgonzola. "Isn't that what ghosts do?"

Chapter Four

That night Hugo Murdock couldn't sleep. Beside him, Melanie snored and made jabbing movements as if she had her umbrella in her hand. Finally, Hugo sat up and looked around. Even though it was pitch black, the room seemed to be full of tiny eyes staring at him.

"What I need is a glass of milk and a biscuit," said Hugo and he went downstairs to the larder. SNAP! OW! Hugo howled as a terrible pain shot through his big toe.

"What's all that noise?" Melanie
shouted down the stairs.

"Did you put down a mousetrap?"
asked Hugo, rubbing at his big red toe.

"Of course not," said Melanie. "There
aren't any mice, remember?"

The next morning Hugo woke in
a bad mood with a sore toe and
a headache.

In the kitchen, Melanie was furious. "You and your midnight snacks! Why did you leave cereal all over the table last night?" she shouted.

"I didn't," said Hugo as he opened *Drill Bits*, his favourite magazine. His jaw dropped. A row of paper dollies had been chewed out of the inside pages.

"Why did you cut up my magazine?"
yelled Hugo.

"I haven't touched your magazine,"
cried Melanie.

"Then it must be mice," said Hugo.

"There–aren't–any–MICE," said
Melanie, spitting out each word.
"Anyway, why on earth would a mouse
chew dollies in your magazine?"

Hugo shook his head. Put like that it did sound rather unlikely, but then who did do it? And who put the trap near the larder? He found himself looking suspiciously at his wife again.

On top of the fridge, the ghost mice started to laugh and a high silvery sound floated in the air.

"What was that?" snapped Melanie.

"Birds," muttered Hugo.

Chapter Five

After breakfast Hugo got ready to go
outside to dig up the rose garden.

"Darling," said Melanie. "There's a
cake-decorating competition in the
village hall. I thought I might enter."

Hugo beamed. "Great idea, sweetest,"
he said. "You'll win, of course."

"Of course," said Melanie. "But I shall
have to bake my cake this afternoon,
so you'll have to do the garden on
your own."

"Okay," said Hugo in a sulky voice.

By teatime, Hugo was in a temper. His
hands were scratched to shreds and he
was filthy dirty.

In the kitchen Melanie was admiring the cake she had just made. It was heart-shaped and on the top was a stagecoach, pulled by four sugar mice. A princess was driving the coach and hitting the mice with a tiny gold whip.

"It's my best ever," murmured Melanie to herself as Hugo stomped through the door. "Oh, there you are, Darling! I need you to put that shelf up in the bedroom for me now."

But Hugo was wrapping a bandage around his hand. "Where's my tea?" he demanded.

"Still in the cupboard," snapped Melanie. "Same place as your drill!"

"What's he doing now?" whispered Gorgonzola from inside a box of Hugo's power tools.

"Getting some biscuits," said Pipsqueak who was on lookout.

Ten minutes later, Hugo put down his mug of tea and lifted his favourite drill from its box. He pushed the start button. Nothing happened.

"Melanie," said Hugo. "Why doesn't my drill work?"

"How on earth should I know?" snapped Melanie.

Hugo turned the drill upside down. The cable was broken. Melanie must have caught it in the door when she was putting the tools away.

"Melanie!" he yelled as he looked in his box. "You've broken the cables on all of my tools."

"Don't be ridiculous, Hugo," said Melanie. "I never touched your tools."

"Well, somebody has," said Hugo, "and it can't have been mi…"

Suddenly, he heard the high silvery sound again and this time it seemed to be coming from inside the cupboard.

"Melanie," said Hugo nervously.

"Have you noticed anything peculiar about this cottage?"

"You're the only peculiar thing," said Melanie and turned back to her cake.

In the cupboard Gorgonzola hugged herself. "It's working!" she cried. "We're winning!"

"I really hope so," said Cheddar. "Have you seen the cake she's made?" And he described everything down to the tiny gold whip.

Gorgonzola felt herself go hot under her fur. "We will show no mercy," she cried. "These strangers will wish they had never set eyes on our cottage."

Later that evening Melanie banged two cups of cocoa on the table.

"I've been thinking about what you said," she muttered. "Maybe we should lock ourselves in tonight."

Hugo walked over to the hook where the key was supposed to be. But there was nothing there.

"It's probably fallen down behind the chest of drawers," said Melanie.

Hugo bent down and fumbled around on the floor.

SNAP! OW! Hugo howled and pulled back his hand. A mousetrap was swinging from his bandaged thumb!

Behind him there was a low choking sound. It was Melanie laughing.

"You did that on purpose," yelped Hugo, his face purple with rage.

"I didn't! I didn't!" cried Melanie, tears pouring down her cheeks. "I promise I didn't!"

36

Chapter Six

"I'm sorry I laughed at you," said Melanie, as she climbed into bed. "I couldn't help it. Something about this place is giving me the jitters."

Hugo tried to put his arm around her but his hand hurt too much. "I know what you mean," he said. "I keep thinking I'm being watched."

"I keep hearing things," said Melanie. "The problem is, if I didn't know better, I'd swear it was mice."

Hugo thought of the tiny bright eyes and the strange silvery laughter. "Maybe the place is haunted," he said. "Some old cottages are, you know."

"But nobody has lived here for over a hundred years," said Melanie.

"Except a whole lot of mice," said Hugo in a hollow voice. "Ghost mice." "There's no such thing as ghost mice," said Melanie, blowing out the candle. "Let's go to sleep. The cake competition is in the morning and the bulldozers are coming."

Two minutes later she was snoring like a cow full of custard.

"Did you hear what she said?" whispered Crackers.

Cheddar nodded. "We'd better tell Gorgonzola."

Gorgonzola called another meeting. "They've got to go by tomorrow morning," she said. "Or Honeycomb Cottage will be destroyed."

"I've got an idea," said Crackers.

"I've got one, too," said Cheddar.

The two mice whispered in Gorgonzola's ears. As they spoke a huge smile spread across her face.

*

"Hugo!" said Melanie. "Wake up!"

Hugo opened his eyes. It was pitch black. "What's going on?" he muttered.

"It's morning," spluttered Melanie. "The window has been blacked out."

Hugo stumbled downstairs. Every window in the house had been covered with pieces of board!

He turned the handle on the front door and pushed. The door was locked. But how? There was an ear-splitting scream behind him. Melanie was standing in the larder in her nightdress, shining a torch at her cake. Hugo gasped with horror.

Melanie's cake had been chewed away. The stagecoach and the princess had disappeared and, in its place, stood a mouse with its arms flexed like a superhero. It had the look of a mouse that had won a great battle.

Melanie's face was as grey as a wasp's nest. She thought of the mousetrap in the front of the larder and the one under the chest of drawers. She thought of the dollies chewed in Hugo's magazine and, last of all, she thought of the monster that had appeared on top of her beautiful cake.

"Hugo," croaked Melanie. "You're right. This cottage is haunted."

"By mice?"

"By mice," whispered Melanie.

They sat in stunned silence staring at each other.

"Hugo?" whispered Melanie again.

"Yes, dear?"

"GET ME OUT OF HERE!"

"The problem is we're, um, locked in."

"Locked in! Locked in!" yelled

Melanie. "I won't be caged in my own cottage like some, some…"

"Mouse?" said Hugo.

Melanie picked up a hammer and smashed it against the front door.

"Come in," said Simon Slime in a silly voice from the other side. "I mean, can I come in?"

Melanie whacked the door again. "Let us out, you idiot," she yelled.

Simon Slime looked down. The big key was on the doorstep. Light burst into the darkened room as the door opened.

"I say," sniggered Simon Slime. "It's rather like a mouse hole in here."

"It IS a mouse hole," shouted Melanie. "And it's haunted by ghost mice!" She picked up her handbag. "We're leaving and we're never coming back."

44

Before Simon Slime could reply, the door slammed shut. Melanie and Hugo were gone.

Simon Slime looked around the kitchen. Nothing much seemed to have changed. He knocked out the boards blocking up the windows and picked up the Honeycomb Cottage sign.

"He's putting it back up," cried Gorgonzola, and all the other mice laughed and cheered.

Simon Slime shivered as he turned the big key in the lock. A most peculiar sound was coming from behind the stove. It was high and silvery like the jingling of little bells. All the ghost mice were laughing with delight.

"We've won at last," cried Gorgonzola. "Honeycomb Cottage is ours again!"

If you enjoyed this story, why not read another *Skylarks* book?

Muffin

by Anne Rooney and Sean Julian

One day, Caitlin finds a baby bird sitting in a broken eggshell. She takes the bird home to the lighthouse and decides to call him Muffin. Muffin is very happy being fed tasty slivers of fish and sleeping in the cosy sock Caitlin has given him, but the time comes when every baby bird must learn to look after itself and Caitlin has to set Muffin free…

Yasmin's Parcels
by Jill Atkins and Lauren Tobia

Yasmin lives in a tiny house with her mama and papa and six little brothers and sisters. They are poor and hungry and, as the oldest child, Yasmin knows she needs to do something to help. So, she sets off to find some food. But Yasmin can't find any food and, instead, is given some mysterious parcels. How can these parcels help her feed her family?

Skylarks titles include:

Awkward Annie
by Julia Williams and Tim Archbold
HB 9780237533847
PB 9780237534028

Sleeping Beauty
by Louise John and Natascia Ugliano
HB 9780237533861
PB 9780237534042

Detective Derek
by Karen Wallace and Beccy Blake
HB 9780237533885
PB 9780237534066

Hurricane Season
by David Orme and Doreen Lang
HB 9780237533892
PB 9780237534073

Spiggy Red
by Penny Dolan and Cinzia Battistel
HB 9780237533854
PB 9780237534035

London's Burning
by Pauline Francis and Alessandro
Baldanzi
HB 9780237533878
PB 9780237534059

The Black Knight
by Mick Gowar and Graham Howells
HB 9780237535803
PB 9780237535926

Ghost Mouse
by Karen Wallace and Beccy Blake
HB 9780237535827
PB 9780237535940

Yasmin's Parcels
by Jill Atkins and Lauren Tobia
HB 9780237535858
PB 9780237535971

Muffin
by Anne Rooney and Sean Julian
HB 9780237535810
PB 9780237535933

Tallulah and the Tea Leaves
by Louise John and Vian Oelofsen
HB 9780237535841
PB 9780237535964

The Big Purple Wonderbook
by Enid Richemont and Kelly Waldek
HB 9780237535834
PB 9780237535957